88   89   92 93   94

/ /)   97

95   96

THE CUCKOO CLOCK

MARY STOLZ

THE CUCKOO CLOCK

ILLUSTRATED BY PAMELA JOHNSON

David R. Godine • Publisher • Boston

Published in 1987 by
David R. Godine, Publisher, Inc.
Horticultural Hall
300 Massachusetts Avenue
Boston, Massachusetts 02115

LIBRARY OF CONGRESS CATALOGING IN PUBLICATION DATA

Stolz, Mary, 1920–
The cuckoo clock.
SUMMARY: Orphaned Erich's life as an unloved drudge
begins to change when old Ula, the town's most skill-
ful clockmaker, takes him on as his helper.
[1. Clocks and watches—Fiction. 2. Magic—
Fiction. 3. Orphans—Fiction] I. Johnson, Pamela, ill.
II. Title.
PZ7.S875854Cu 1987 [Fic] 86-45538
ISBN 0-87923-653-1

FIRST EDITION

Printed in the United States of America

Written for Eileen and Margie

THE CUCKOO CLOCK

Once upon a time, there lived a clockmaker in a village at the edge of the Black Forest in Germany. Long ago he had been known as Young Ula, the clockmaker. Then as Ula, the clockmaker. In time, he became Old Ula, the clockmaker.

For years past numbering, he had been the finest maker of the famous Black Forest cuckoo clock anywhere in the world. When the best was wanted in the way of such a clock, people came to Ula. Travelers from across the oceans, when they were near the Black Forest, stopped at his village to order a clock from him.

Some, when they heard how long it was going to take, went away without ordering. Angry. Or disappointed. Anyway, not patient.

"To make a clock takes time," Ula would say, looking to see whether his customer appreciated the little joke. "To make a clock takes a good deal of *time*."

Old Ula's clocks were entirely hand-made. The workings were old-fashioned and simple. Four wheels in each train, verge escapements and foliot. He always began with the works. Carving the wooden wheels and spindles, fashioning the two long chains of brass links, fashioning the bellows and the wire gong that would give the bird its voice. He cast two weights of lead, in the form of fir cones. Then he would proceed to the dial face, carving lacy hands and numerals. Then he would make the house. Small, sometimes. Sometimes large. Usually something between small and large.

But never simple.

The workings of his clocks were so severe and plain that nothing ever went wrong with them. But the cases, the houses that surrounded these works, were of the most elaborate kind.

Naturally, people ordering a clock made by hand by the finest clockmaker in the Black Forest directed what they wished to have in the way of decoration. And usually they wished to display on the face of the clock their skill as hunters.

For instance, one day Baron Balloon came into the clockmaker's small cottage. Baron Balloon himself lived in a castle at the top of a mountain from which he could look down on the village. Sometimes he did not come off his peak for weeks. But today he had ordered the carriage with its coachman and span of gray horses, and down the winding road he'd come, especially to commission the finest, largest, most intricate and imposing cuckoo clock that Old Ula had ever made. It was to be a present for his daughter at Christmas, now four months away.

Brangi, the clockmaker's big brown dog, was lying

across the doorstep in the sunlight. Brangi was getting old. Once he had frolicked through fields and forest, and fought other dogs, and loved other dogs. He had bayed at the moon with a full deep voice. But of late he preferred to lie on the doorstep in the warm sun, or lie beside the hearth in the evening by the leaping fire. The moon no longer called to him.

Now he was in the Baron's way.

The Baron, accustomed to having everyone and everything get out of his way, stopped at the doorstep and said, "Hoh! Move!"

Brangi thumped his tail and sighed and relaxed. He hadn't a notion of what was due a Baron in the way of obedience. The Baron's own dogs jumped when he snapped his fingers, but they'd been trained by their parents.

Brangi just lolled there, blocking the Baron's entrance.

"Hoh, Ula!" the Baron bellowed. "Get this hound out of my path, or I shall be obliged to have my coachman remove him!"

Ula, who had been growing rather deaf, had not heard the arrival of the Baron's coach, but now he rose from his workbench and shuffled to the door.

"Come, Brangi," he said mildly. "Don't you know an important man when you're lying across his path?"

Brangi glanced up, yawned, seemed to reflect, and, just as the Baron was on the point of bellowing again, moved slowly into the cottage, where he subsided on a rug beside the clockmaker's worktable, put his head on his paws, and went to sleep.

"And now, Herr Baron," said Ula. "What may I do for you?"

The Baron looked about the room. Accustomed as he was to castles, it seemed pretty poor stuff to him. A room with a workbench at one end, beneath a window. A fireplace with a box settle to one side and an old rocker to the other. A hooked rug. White curtains at the windows. Several clocks on the wall, finished and waiting to be picked up by those who had ordered them. Two on the workbench, undergoing repairs.

There was a longcase clock in one corner. "Did you make that?" the Baron demanded, pointing.

"Alas, no. I make only cuckoo clocks. That was made by a friend, now gone."

"You bought it from him?" said the Baron in surprise. It was a clock, obviously, of great value.

"He gave it to me."

"Hmph. It's an exceedingly fine one." Its fineness irritated the Baron. He had bought a great many things in his life, but had never been *given* anything. He considered offering to buy it, looked at the clockmaker and reconsidered.

He continued his haughty inspection of the cottage, but there was nothing more to see, except a staircase going up one wall to the clockmaker's bedroom, and, at one side of the workbench, Erich the Foundling, carefully sanding a spindle.

"Tell that boy to leave," ordered the Baron Balloon.

Old Ula smiled and shook his head. "Not possible, Mein Herr. He is my assistant."

Erich the Foundling lowered his glance proudly, but he was alarmed. The Baron was so huge and important and loud, and Old Ula so gentle and quiet.

"You, boy—out!" said the Baron.

Erich the Foundling, used to obeying orders, started from the bench, but Old Ula said again, "Not possible, Herr Baron. Remain where you are, Erich. And now, Herr Baron, tell me. Is there something I can do for you?"

"You can begin by heeding my order."

"Oh, dear." Old Ula shook his head regretfully. "Then our business is concluded before it is begun. You must understand, Herr Baron, that I do not heed orders from other men. I obey my stomach when it demands to be fed, and my body when it asks to be put to bed, and my heart when it bids me love—" He glanced at Erich. "I shall obey my God, when he summons me from here. But as to obeying you—" He sighed. "No, I fear that will not be possible."

The Baron turned and made for the cottage door in noisy fury; then he paused, waiting for Ula to plead with him not to leave. As no words came, he stomped back into the room. "What I have to do here with you is a matter of great *secrecy*. I propose a splendid gift for my daughter—" He stopped again, looking expectant.

Old Ula said, "A beautiful girl, Mein Herr." He did not mind saying this, even though the Baron expected him to, because Britt, the Baron's daughter, was indeed a beautiful girl. Just about Erich's age, thought Ula. Ten. Ten years, for her, of being made to feel the center of the world. Ten years, for Erich, of wondering where in the world he had come from, where in it he belonged.

Under such difficult, very different, circumstances, they were both nice children. Old Ula found this wonderful to contemplate.

"I think that Erich and I," he said, "will be able to keep your secret."

"Oh, very well then," said the Baron with bad grace. "This is what I want. You are to make for me, by Christmas, the finest, largest, most intricate and imposing cuckoo clock that ever has been. This is how I wish the decorations to be . . . write down what I say!"

"I can remember."

"How can I be sure of that? You are an old man. You might forget some detail."

Brangi, who had begun to dislike the sound of the Baron's voice, got to his feet with a low snarl. Old Ula put a hand on the dog's head, fondled his ears. "Herr Baron, I have a suggestion."

"And what may that be?"

"There is Fritz, the young clockmaker, at the other end of the village. I am sure that he would write down everything you say, and would make you a fine clock. He is going to be—that is to say, he *is*—a fine workman. But I could not possibly finish a clock for you, even of the simplest, by Christmas. To make a clock takes *time*."

Again the Baron started for the door, again wheeled and stomped back into the room. Fritz was a good clockmaker, but everyone knew that Old Ula was the best anywhere. And for the Baron's daughter, even the best would scarcely serve. He would give it to her for her birthday, in April. Surely even this stubborn old man could get the fanciest clock done by then.

Breathing heavily, the Baron said, "You are to make this clock precisely as I say, forgetting nothing. Do you understand?"

"I understand what you have said."

The Baron, taking this for agreement, continued. "The

entire face of the house is to be decorated, every inch. *And,* mind you, the sides!" He looked triumphantly at Old Ula. "What do you think of that, eh? Never thought of decorating the sides, have you?"

"In fact, I have, upon occasion, done this."

"Old man, you are deliberately trying to annoy me!"

"No, no, no . . . not at all. I should never dream of trying to annoy a Baron."

Baron Balloon looked at the clockmaker suspiciously, but saw only an open, frank, friendly, wrinkled face. Were the eyes a shade merry?

"For two *pfennigs* I'd go to Munich over this business," he growled. The clockmaker remained silent. The Baron scowled. Erich looked at the floor. Brangi yawned.

"Very well," the Baron resumed. "I shall wait until April. My daughter's birthday is on the eighteenth of April. The clock must be ready by then. Understood? Now, to the decorations . . . a stag's head, with five-branched antlers to surmount the whole, with a large bow and arrow just beneath. It was with a bow and arrow that I brought down my finest beast. You may come up to the castle and sketch his head. Down one side I wish a brace of geese to hang by their feet, and on the other a brace of hare. Fowling pieces on each side, fit them how you will. At the bottom, stretched at length, a wild boar—"

"Dead?"

"Of course, dead. With large tusks. Hunting rifles to each side of him. And, old man, just see here—I have brought you the skull of a little doe to be used for the pendulum bob. Is it not beautiful?"

The clockmaker thought the slender skull was indeed

a pretty thing, but he lifted a hand to prevent Baron Balloon from putting it on the workbench.

"Effective, hah?" said the Baron, tossing the little skull from one hand to the other. "As to the rest of the clock case, fill it in with more hunting gear, also doves, geese, rabbits. These can look as if they had not yet been killed. A few vines, some leaves. You'll know what I mean, but make sure every inch is carved in some manner. I want this to be such a clock as has never been seen before, anywhere."

"Herr Baron—"

Being interrupted one moment and not replied to the next was beginning to get on the Baron's nerves. How he longed for the old days—distant, but still current in his family's stories—the feudal days, when a man like this Ula would scarcely dare lift his eyes to a Baron's.

"Well, what is it?" he snapped. "Get on with it. I am in a vast hurry."

Old Ula, who was not in a hurry, looked about his little cottage for a few moments longer.

"It is this way, Baron Balloon," he said at length. "I am, as you have observed several times, an old man. But mark you, Mein Herr, an old person has one great advantage over a young one who is still pressing forward, striving to do, to be, to get, to grow rich or grow famous, to command and to possess. I have no interest in these matters. And—I come to the point—I have decided to make a clock for myself."

In fact, this notion, which had only come upon him since the Baron's arrival, now seized his imagination, and he marveled that he had not thought of it before. It would be, of course, his last clock. Already his hands were beginning to stiffen, his fingers to ache. But he felt they would do this last piece of work for him. A clock made by himself, to his own order!

So enchanted was he by the idea that he turned from the Baron to the boy at the table and said, "Look here, Erich, we have no time to lose. We must work hard to repair these two clocks in short, but good, order. And then, my son, why, *then—*"

"Ula!"

The clockmaker turned. "Ah, Herr Baron, excuse me. I forget my manners. May I bid you good day," he said hastily.

The Baron sputtered. *Sputtered!*

"Do you mean to imply—are you meaning to say—is it possible that you are *refusing* to make my clock? The one I came all the way down the mountain to order from you? How dare you refuse me anything? I am the Baron Balloon, and from my castle I look down on the entire village!"

Oh, how he yearned to say, *I own this village!* as his great-great-great-great-great-grandfather would have said.

Old Ula stroked his beard in silence for a while and then said, "That is how it seems to be."

"You refuse?"

"I refuse."

"But this is not possible!"

"Let me explain. I have decided to make a clock for myself, to my own order. I have never done this in all my years of clockmaking. Yes, I shall begin to make my very own clock as soon as these two on the table are set right."

Baron Balloon was beside himself with rage, with outrage, with sheer blistering fury. People did not decline to do what he, the Baron Balloon, wished done! Yet here was this poor, witless, aged, *annoying* man—refusing!

What was more, the Baron saw no way around the problem. The old idiot shimmered with stubbornness. The Baron had seen the same look in the eyes of a mule that had made up its mind not to move.

With another sigh for the days when a Baron's will was law, he said, "Very well, then. How long will it take you to make this clock you are ordering for yourself?"

Old Ula thought. Then he said, "The rest of my life."

Baron Balloon stamped out of the cottage, uttering oaths. He drove across the village to Fritz, the young clock-maker, who eagerly agreed to all the Baron's stipulations, even to having the clock completed by Christmas. He would put aside all other work, put his present customers off, work night as well as day, and he would produce a clock that would put proud Old Ula's work in the shadow.

His mind awhirl with fowling pieces, boars' tusks, doe's-skull pendulum bobs, he could scarcely wait for the Baron to leave so that he could begin work on his master-piece.

At the cottage of Old Ula, Erich the Foundling stared with wide eyes at his ancient friend. "Are you not afraid?" he asked.

"Do you think I should be?"

Erich nodded solemnly. "He is big and powerful, the Baron. He can—he can—"

Ula patted the boy's head in the same soothing manner

as he had patted Brangi's. "You see? You cannot even think of something for me to be afraid of. The Baron huffs and puffs, but can he blow my house in?"

Erich thought the Baron could easily do that. He knew that most people in the village leaped to do his bidding. Certainly the Goddharts, with whom Erich had lived all his life, leaped. Herr Goddhart, whom Erich loved, leaped reluctantly. Frau Goddhart, whom he did not love, leaped promptly. But they were not different from the rest of the villagers.

"Why are you not afraid?" he asked Old Ula curiously.

"Because, as I explained to the Baron Balloon, I am too old to fear anything a man can do to me, and I know my Maker means me only good. So, young Erich, let us set to work on these two infirm clocks and make them healthy again."

Frau Goddhart enjoyed a reputation for kindness.

"*Ach*, Frau Goddhart," people of the village would say, "she is the *soul* of kindness."

Let anyone fall sick, and there was Frau Goddhart, usually even before the doctor came. Should a family be needy, Frau Goddhart would arrive with clothing and blankets, clean and neatly mended, things no longer wanted at the Goddhart Manor House. A person in trouble found in Frau Goddhart a willing listener. As she explained to Herr Goddhart, a person in trouble often needs a listener more than he needs material aid. She had a pleasant voice, almost as pleasant to her hearers as to herself, and was frequently to be found reading to invalids. She sang in the church choir. She carried sweetmeats in her pocket and gave them to children as she went about the village being the soul of kindness.

A godsend, she was called.

Frau Goddhart sometimes found the burden of her

reputation heavy to bear. She rejoiced in it, but it weighed upon her. Nobody, she reasoned, could be expected to be kindly *all* the time.

And so, within the walls of the Manor House, she let slip the yoke. She snapped at her husband, snarled at the children, bullied the servants. Having been a good listener and a godsend all day in the village, she thought it little enough to expect quiet and obedience at home in the evening.

What Frau Goddhart expected, she got.

When she was at home, the Manor House was quiet. Despite a man, six children, a foundling, and many servants, one might almost have thought the big house deserted as folks tiptoed about and spoke in whispers so as not to disturb Frau Goddhart, resting from a day of charity and compassion.

The snarls she directed at her own children were of an absent-minded, usually quite affectionate order. Those she aimed at Erich the Foundling were genuine. *He* had taken advantage of her reputation for kindness. She had no doubt of that in the world.

It had come about thus:

One morning, ten years before, a bundle with a baby within had been found on Frau Goddhart's doorstep. In the ordinary way of things, in those days, foundlings were found on the church steps. But with Frau Goddhart's renown for benevolence, what was more natural than that the desperate parent should think of this good woman and suppose that her large heart could accommodate an unfortunate waif? She already had six children. Could one more

be in the way? So the unhappy parent who left the baby must have reasoned.

Frau Goddhart had always felt it very hard luck indeed that the bundle had been disclosed in full view of the villagers, all returning from church on a soft spring morning. Had she come out to find it earlier in the day, when no one was about, she would most assuredly have bundled the bundle off to the church steps, where she felt it belonged. But as she and Herr Goddhart and the six young Goddharts approached the Manor House, there it was—a struggling, whimpering bundle of baby. Frau Goddhart was not only offered an opportunity for public kindness, there was no way to avoid it.

"Ach, the poor little one," she exclaimed angrily. Observing many eyes upon her, she continued, lifting her voice and her chin, "It enrages me that a child of God should be cast off in this manner. I shall take the waif in and mother it as one of my own."

Much gratification among the onlookers. Herr Goddhart picked up the blanket-enfolded bellowing baby and held it gently. Its sobs subsided.

"Take the thing—take the *child* into the house," Frau Goddhart directed. "God has sent it to us."

God could easily have sent it to the church, she thought irritably, and it seemed to her unfair that He had chosen to do otherwise.

Consider, just *consider*, all she had done and given in His name! A pipe for the church organ. An aisle runner. The most beautifully embroidered altar cloth in the Black Forest. A stained-glass window! Her lovely singing, week after week! Her visits to the poor! Her—benefices, too many to count!

This was how God rewarded her!

Well, it was not easy to be a woman of extraordinary kindness, not at all easy, she thought, as she accepted this burden that was laid upon her in full view of the village.

The villagers now turned away to their homes. In her mind she could hear their praises. No doubt some would be going too far, calling her a saint. The chorus of their admiration sounded in her mind and made up for much inconvenience.

Once inside the Manor House, Frau Goddhart called one of the maids and informed her that she was to be greatly blessed. She was to have the sole care of this waif of God. The maid, a young girl with little free time, proved stubborn about accepting her good fortune, but Frau Goddhart had little trouble convincing her to accept the ways of Divine Providence. The maids, the grooms, the gardeners, Herr Goddhart, and the six young Goddharts were all afraid of Frau Goddhart. They knew she was a woman of unusual kindness, because everybody said so, and the entire village could not be wrong. They only wondered at how different it seemed to be when she was alone with her household. None of them spoke of her elsewhere in any but the warmest terms. They would not have been believed, to begin with. But, in addition, Frau Goddhart would have found out. She would not be pleased. It seemed best all around to please her. Herr Goddhart occasionally explained to a weeping scullery maid or a fuming groom or a crying small Goddhart that the problem must lie with them. They must not perfectly understand the nature of goodness.

Then he'd step outside the house to smoke his pipe.

Erich the Foundling lived in the attic. In the days of which we speak, foundlings, waifs, orphans, and step-children lived in the attic. As it chanced, Erich quite liked his room under the eaves. The maid into whose care he'd been given had long since gone off with a follower, a young man who laughed a lot. She had explained as she eloped with him on a moonlit summer's night that in all her years at the Manor House she had never heard anyone laugh.

"It gives Frau Goddhart a headache, to hear laughter," she said.

"Now, that's a funny thing," said her young man. "Many's the time I've heard her laughing away on the lawn at the castle." He had been a forester in Baron Balloon's park until he decided to run off with Frau Goddhart's maid in the middle of the night. "But she's a saintly woman, all the same," he said.

"Oh yes, of course," said the little maid, out of habit, and off they went and were never heard of again.

From the age of five, Erich was quite on his own. Except for jobs he was required to do around the Manor House —blacking boots, scouring pots, toting pails of water for the copper hip-tubs in the bedrooms, carrying slops to the pigs, splitting wood for the fires, cleaning out the hearths, scrubbing the stone floors, all tasks normally set to orphans and suchlike in those days—his time was his own, since no one except Herr Goddhart paid him any attention.

He was allowed to attend the other children's lessons,

as nobody ever really noticed that he was there at the back of the schoolroom. So, with Herr Goddhart's occasional present of books, he learned to write and read quite as well as the children of the house. Better than some.

No one came to his attic room. He was free to keep there, openly, the books Herr Goddhart secretly gave him. Herr Goddhart also smuggled him extra candles, so that he could read at night and not have to account for a candle in the morning. The attic room was cozy under the roof, and he had an old eiderdown that was warm in winter.

All in all, Erich was content, but the truth must be told: he *never* played. Until he was eight years old, he was never happy.

As he knew nothing about happiness, the lack of it did not trouble him. He considered himself fortunate, because Frau Goddhart had taken him in. He did not like her, and he decided that when he grew up he would be careful not to be kind. He would be like Herr Goddhart instead. Herr Goddhart was never spoken of in the village as a good man. He was not spoken of at all. He did not make the rounds of the poor with his wife, or visit the Baron and Baroness Balloon with her, or stand beside her while she distributed sweetmeats to the children or listened to people's troubles with an absent-minded but charitable air. In fact, the only time the elder Goddharts were seen together was in church. In the ample shadow of his spouse Herr Goddhart seemed to disappear quite gently. Erich decided that to be quiet and gentle was a better aspiration than to be kind.

One day when he was eight years old, he happened to be patting Ula the clockmaker's dog, Brangi, when Old Ula himself came out on the step to stretch and yawn.

"Ah, Erich," said Old Ula. "You like Brangi?"

"Oh, yes. I like him very very much."

"He seems to take to you. If he were a cat, I believe he would be purring."

Erich smiled.

"You, of course, do not have a dog," Old Ula went on.

"Oh, no. There are dogs at the Manor House, but they belong to the family."

"You are not one of the family?"

"No, Herr Ula. I am a foundling."

"Yes, I know that."

Everyone knew everything about everyone else in the village.

"Well," said Old Ula, "why do you not make Brangi your part-time dog?"

"Could I?"

"Most certainly. That is what he needs, a part-time owner just your age."

Erich sighed, wondering what this odd feeling was that seemed to—to flower within him. Not a feeling he had known before, though it was something akin to being with Herr Goddhart. Times with Herr Goddhart were so rare, so secretive, that he was never able to be glad at them for wondering when they would stop. Frau Goddhart would call her husband, and of course he always left off anything he was doing when Frau Goddhart called. Being with Herr Goddhart was the best feeling Erich had known, but not a secure one.

Now, with Old Ula and Brangi, there was no sense of hurry, no uneasy waiting for a voice to summon them away. Indeed, Old Ula and his dog seemed to have all the time in the world. The dog lay on his back, letting Erich scratch his stomach. Ula sat on the step in the sunshine and smoked his pipe. The hollyhocks stirred in the warm summer breeze.

Later, Erich knew that what he had felt then was happiness, but at the time he did not trouble to wonder further. He just sat there with the old man and the dog in the sunshine, feeling peaceful.

Presently Old Ula knocked the ashes of his pipe in the palm of his hand, scattered them among the hollyhocks, and stood up. Brangi got to his feet. Erich looked at them uncertainly. He supposed he had better make his way back to the Manor House and his chores.

"I am about to prepare a cup of chocolate," said Old Ula. "Would you care to have some with me?"

Erich hesitated. He knew he should be starting back, but could not—simply could not—refuse a chance to be a little longer in the company of Old Ula and Brangi. Perhaps if he had the chocolate and then *ran* all the way back—

"Thank you, Mein Herr," he said. "I should like that."

"Then come in, come in. And call me Ula, for a favor."

"Yes. Yes, thank you, Herr Ula."

"No, no, no. *Ula.* Call me Ula. I am so old and you are so young that we can dispense with formalities, is that not so?"

"Oh, yes," Erich the Foundling said softly. "We can, we can."

In the cottage, while Old Ula prepared the chocolate, with a plate of ginger cookies made by himself, Erich looked curiously at the tools on the workbench. There were knives with knurled handles and blades of different shapes—some tapered, some thick, long ones and short. There were pliers and wood drills, vises, cutting broaches, stiff bristled brushes, coarse and fine sanders, a wooden anvil, a box full of brass chain links. Mysterious and dazzling sights to a boy who had never touched any tool except a shovel!

"You find them interesting, eh?" said his host.

Erich nodded. "The knives are so shiny and sharp and ready to work. And these other things—all these strange things that I don't know the names of—"

Old Ula picked up various implements and explained their use. Finally he drew toward him a soft leather sack that he unrolled to reveal a set of knives, chisels, gauges, and a small silver hammer. They flashed in the sunlight from the window as Old Ula hefted them, one after the other, in his palm.

"My finest carving tools. For work on the finest clocks, those with the most delicate and intricate relief. A workman's tools are wonderful things, Erich. They are, I think you can say, part of him. Not just more fingers, but part of his being. I speak of tools, you understand. Not of these machines that are coming into use, that are driven by power and not by the man himself. For machines I have no use."

"Oh, but a machine could never make a clock!" Erich exclaimed, so excited at having a real conversation that he dared to interrupt. "That can never be."

"Here now, have your chocolate and let us speak of less terrible things. For instance, I could use a helper here. How would you like the job?"

Erich's eyes and mouth opened wide. He could not speak at all.

"I take that to mean yes?" said Old Ula. "That expression of huge surprise?"

Erich let his breath out. "I do not think, Herr Ula—I mean, Ula—that Frau Goddhart would permit it. She wants me at the Manor House."

"She cherishes you so much?"

Erich the Foundling shook his head. "No," he said seriously. "But still, I do not think—"

"We shall see, we shall see. More chocolate, another cookie?"

The next day Old Ula presented himself at the Goddhart Manor House and asked if Frau Goddhart could spare
him a moment.

She came into the great hall, looking merciful. Old Ula,
who worked so slowly and never charged enough for his
clocks, had no doubt fallen on hard times. He was here to
beg a few clothes, a few *pfennigs*, a fowl for his kettle.
When they kept their petitions modest, Frau Goddhart often
obliged the villagers in such ways.

"And now you, Ula," said Frau Goddhart, as if he were
part of a horde of supplicants, although except for the two
of them the vast hall was empty. "What is your trouble?"

"Nothing at all, Frau Goddhart. Oh, the joints ache a
little—"

"I have a salve and will give you a small pot." She
reached for the bell-pull to summon a servant.

"I have some salve," said Old Ula. "Thank you all the
same."

"But then—"

"I have come about the boy, Erich."

Frau Goddhart's kindly mouth tightened. "What has he done? If there are damages, mind—"

"No, no, no," said Old Ula impatiently. "Nothing like that. I am come to inquire whether you would permit him to work as my assistant."

"Your assistant? The boy isn't even bright."

This was so far from true that Old Ula judged it better not to comment.

"He would start with the simplest tasks, I assure you, Frau Goddhart."

"You would not expect him to be at your cottage much of the day? He is required here—that is to say, we could not spare his dear company for too long at a time."

Old Ula had the effect on people that they slipped their pretenses with him. It was one of the reasons he and Brangi spent much of their time alone—people's pretenses being, of course, important to them.

Frau Goddhart drew hers about her. She let it be known, in the most gracious fashion, that for Erich's own good he must continue with his chores here at the Manor House.

"After all," she said sadly, "with six children of our own, we cannot make any provision for the lad, but are doing the best we can by providing him with the training of a good household servant. He may be lucky enough, in a couple of years, to find a place with my friend, the Baroness. I shall use my influence."

"How good of you," said Old Ula. "On the other hand, should he learn to be a clockmaker—"

"You cannot mean to take him on as your apprentice?" said Frau Goddhart, not adding that since an apprenticeship took seven years there was little chance that Ula would be around to see Erich through it.

"No. Unhappily, not as an apprentice. But he could learn a few things while with me, and then just possibly go to young Fritz, if in your great benevolence you saw fit to release—that is, to allow him to undertake such an apprenticeship."

Frau Goddhart was of two minds. Erich the Foundling had always been a thorn in her side. He had not proved a credit to her, being thin and silent, like a reproach, not plump and lively like her own children. Still, he was extremely useful backstairs, and gave the servants, whom she bullied for their own good, someone to bully in turn. That was always a satisfactory situation.

"Well, no need to look so far ahead," she said. "We must think what is best for the boy. Meanwhile, he can go to your cottage for a portion of each day. Say, from the hour before noon until two hours after. This will leave him time to do wholesome work about the Manor House."

It would also oblige Old Ula to give the foundling lunch, making one mouth less to feed at home. Frau Goddhart could not help it, she really did grudge Erich his meals. Taking, as it were, food out of the mouths of her own children. She had never said this, but her eye was on Erich when he ate—one reason, doubtless, why Erich was thin and the Goddhart children plump.

So it came about that Erich the Foundling spent three hours of each day with Ula and Brangi, learning what the clockmaker's tools were for. Learning how gradual and delicate was the fashioning of a fine clock. How the making of a clock took *time*. He was permitted to handle the tools. Not, Old Ula explained carefully, the first, finest set—the sharp and gleaming instruments that he himself used—but the second set, which had been his when he was an apprentice himself, many, many years before.

Erich was encouraged to whittle on scraps of wood. He was allowed to cast the weights, sand the wooden spindles. But he did not, in fact, do much work. Mostly he listened and watched, and by the time he was ten years old he could have told anyone how to make a cuckoo clock, though he could not have made one himself.

"You will, you will," said Old Ula, as they sat one day at the workbench, doing repairs on two clocks already overdue. Ula would not hurry, which was why young Fritz was getting more and more business. "You will be a fine clockmaker one day. Has Frau Goddhart said anything to you about being apprenticed to Fritz?"

"But Ula! I do not want to be apprenticed to Fritz. I want to stay here with you."

"And so you shall, for as long as it is possible."

"Why should it ever be impossible?" Erich cried out.

Old Ula patted his head and said, "Never mind, never mind, nothing to worry about just yet, let us get back to work here."

He was fashioning a little coiled spring, and Erich was sanding a spindle, and Brangi was lying across the doorway in the sun, when the Baron Balloon arrived.

· · ·

The two sick clocks were rapidly brought around to good health, to the surprise of their owners, who had resigned themselves to months of delay. Although he paid these two proper respect and attention, Ula's thoughts were entirely on his latest, and last, commission, the clock he had ordered for himself.

He began, as always, with the works, carving the escapements, then the wheels and spindles, which he gave to Erich for careful sanding. He fashioned the bellows and the wire gong, and the two long chains of brass links. Together he and Erich cast the lead weights shaped like fir cones. As each piece was finished, it was put aside on the workbench.

The bench was also their dining table, a small part of it at one end being where Old Ula and Erich sat to their lunch of bread and cheese and apples and—most wonderful of all to Erich—chocolate, and ginger cookies. While Old Ula smoked his pipe, right there in the house, Erich would eat and eat. He, who had always gone about with his bones sticking out, began to put on a little weight. While they ate, they discussed the clock. Then they cleared the dishes, got out the books, and Erich's lessons began.

He had only three hours at Old Ula's house each day, and shortly after he began coming there, he had been advanced, at the Manor House, from blacking boots and carrying slops for the pigs and scouring pots and splitting wood and so forth to being an under-gardener under the under-gardener who was under the head vegetable gardener. That is to say, he still blacked boots, scoured pots, carried slops for the pigs, split wood, and so forth, but he was also permitted to work long hours under the under-gardener in the vast vegetable gardens belonging to the Manor House. He weeded and hoed and sowed and reaped according to the under-gardener's instructions, and by the time he reached his attic room at night, Erich was too tired to use Herr Goddhart's extra candles for reading by.

"Do you still read before you go to sleep?" Old Ula had asked one day.

Erich shook his head. "I am too tired. Besides, dear Ula, I no longer go to the classroom, as Frau Goddhart says I may not waste time both here *and* there." He frowned a little. "That is what she says."

"I see. Well, Erich, we shall have to change our schedule. No, no, no . . . do not be alarmed. What I have in mind is that when you come in the morning you will help me with the clocks, and then after lunch I shall teach you other things. Would you like that, eh?"

"Oh, very very much," said Erich. "What would you teach me?"

"Let me see. Well, we shall do sums one day, and study the geography of the world the next, and do reading and writing on the next three. That leaves two days. How would you like to learn to play the fiddle?"

Old Ula had a fiddle hanging on his wall, and from time to time he would take it down and play for Brangi and Erich little airs by Mozart, and Palestrina, and Lully, and others. He would tell Erich stories about the lives of these musicians.

Erich thought that, next to learning to be a clockmaker, what he would most like in the world was to be able to play the fiddle.

And he did learn to play it. It was the only playing he ever did in his life, but all his life he thought it grander than any game.

In later years, Erich thought that he had really learned everything he knew during those three hours each day he spent with Old Ula, the clockmaker. But after the visit from Baron Balloon, when the two clocks had been well repaired and dispatched to their owners, Erich and Ula found they could not put their minds on the lessons.

They could think only of the clock—*the clock*!

"It is to be a forest sonata," Old Ula explained, sketching the design for the case. "Leaves and vines and birds' nests with eggs in some and nestlings in others, and fledglings on twigs. I shall carve a springing doe at the peak, and any number of birds that appear to fly and rabbits that seem to leap and wildflowers that seem to spring from the very wood of the case. The bob will be a moon with two storks passing in front. . . ."

Spellbound, Erich watched sketches flow from a pencil held in the gnarled fingers. When they'd completed the works, before he got to the actual carving of the case, Old Ula made a tin dial with lacy carved tin hands. He painted the hands bright yellow and the dial-face a pale leaf-green with a border of flowers.

The night before Old Ula was to begin work on the case that would house his bird, Erich stayed up very late. He was tired, but not sleepy. Sitting at the window of his attic room, the eiderdown wrapped around him, he looked out at the village. Snow was falling on steep roofs, on steeples, on dark cobbled streets. It fell on great nests perched atop chimneys.

The nests were empty now. In summer, storks raised their families on rooftops all over town, but now the storks were in Africa. Erich knew this from his lessons with Ula. The storks were in Africa, and snow fell into the empty nests while smoke from fires below rose through them like ribbons streaming upwards.

Erich sat up until only here and there did the lamplight from a window spill into the whirling snow. Then he got into bed and fell asleep and dreamed about the clock. This was not unusual. Nearly every night he dreamed about the clock. But his dream tonight was strange and marvelous, and the next day he ran all the way to the clockmaker's, his breath frosty on the brittle air, his boots squeaking in the snow.

"Ula!" he called, bursting into the cottage. "Ula! I must tell you my dream!"

Old Ula looked at him with surprise. "Now, that is surely a strange thing. I was waiting for you to arrive so that I could tell you mine."

Erich sat on the rug beside Brangi and said, "But then I can tell mine, too, all right?"

"Oh, but yours must come first, since you ran with it all the way through the snowy village."

"*Well*," said Erich, taking a deep breath. "*Well* . . . I dreamed that we made a house *inside* the cuckoo clock, a little house just like this one you live in, for the bird to live in. And I dreamed that our—your—yes, *our* bird lived in there and had chocolate and cookies and sat beside the fire and at night went up to his bedroom that was just like your bedroom and read in a little wooden book and then went to

sleep in his four-post bed just like your bed—" He stopped, breathless.

"And I dreamed," said Old Ula, "that our bird was not a cuckoo—or, at least, he looked like a cuckoo, but sang a song no cuckoo knows. He was like a mockingbird, and he sang all the songs of the other birds of the Black Forest—"

"And he flew around out here, and he landed on your shoulder and on Brangi's head and on my hand, and he sang, sang, sang. . . ."

They looked at each other, the old man and the boy, and realized that they had shared the same dream, which was a remarkable thing and made them happy.

"Then let us begin on the house," said Old Ula, "and on the house within the house."

For the case, he planned to use black walnut, a tree from the Forest. It is a hard wood, and the work of carving would go forward slowly. But for the little house inside, he chose pine. This is a softer wood, and Erich helped work with it.

Ula built the two rooms, the downstairs room and a little staircase leading to the bedroom upstairs with a tiny dormer window in it, just like his own. He pegged the floors, carved out a fireplace for upstairs and one for downstairs. He used scraps of orange and yellow silk for the fires.

Erich, who had learned to use some of the tools with dexterity, carved a little box settle, a workbench, a rocker, a four-post bed. He braided a little rug for the downstairs room and sewed a white counterpane for the four-post bed. He made a little table to go beside the bed, and a lamp and even a tiny wooden book to go on the table. Old Ula aways had his Bible on the table beside the bed, so the bird would have his Bible, too.

Then work on the case began.

As Old Ula had predicted, it went slowly. In the morning, when Erich arrived, he would find Ula working, just as he had left him working the afternoon before.

"Do you ever sleep, Ula?" he asked one day.

"Oh, surely. But as we grow older, Brangi and I, he sleeps more and I sleep less. I need this time to work in. Brangi does not care about time or clocks. He cares for sleep, for food, for you and me, eh?"

Brangi, hearing himself spoken of, got to his feet and wagged his tail. Slowly.

Ula smiled, and then said, "Look, Erich—last night I began a covey of quail down in the corner here. What think you?"

Erich thought this clock, as it took shape, was the most magnificent thing he had ever seen. He thought, and he was right, that he would not see its like again.

The creatures—the springing doe, the rabbits and hares, the geese, pheasants and quail, the birds in their nests, birds fledging and flying, the very petals of the wildflowers with their weedy stems—all seemed to quiver with life. It seemed to Erich that Ula did not so much carve as bring the birds and beasts and flowers forth from the wood, as if these wild wonderful lives had been in there all the time, waiting for the magic of Ula's hands.

Erich did no work on the housing. While Old Ula carved, he would play softly on the fiddle the airs from Mozart, Palestrina, and Lully that Ula had taught him.

He played songs that the children of the village sang.

Kuckuk, Kuckuk, ruft's aus dem Wald . . . (Cuckoo, cuckoo, it calls out of the woods . . .)

Or, *Röslein, röslein, röslein rot, röslein auf der Heide* . . . (Wild rose, wild rose, wild rose red, wild rose of the woodland . . .)

Pretty tunes, to please Old Ula as he leaned near-sightedly over the clock case, sculpting a rose, a wing. . . .

One day Ula finished carving the two storks flying past the moon, and the pendulum bob was complete. He leaned back, studying the work of all these past months.

"What say you, Erich? What do you say to our clock, now that it is finished, save only for a bird to live in it?"

Erich put the fiddle down and walked over to the work-bench. He blinked back tears. It was so beautiful, so vivid, so close to coming alive. Any moment, he felt, the doe would leap into the room and out of the door, the geese and quail and doves would fly away, the rabbits and the hares and the little wild boar bound from the waving weeds, past Brangi's nose, out into the forest where they belonged.

"But Ula," he said, after a long while, "down here in the corner. There is an empty space next to the covey of quail!"

"Ah," said Ula the clockmaker, "that space is for you to fill in, my son."

"Me? Carve? On your clock?"

"Our clock, Erich. This is something we have created together, and I daresay there will never be another like it in the world." Unrolling the soft leather sack, he gestured at his finest tools. "Take what you need, and carve what you like."

Trembling, Erich selected a tapering knife, a small chisel, and the silver hammer. He approached the clock, held his breath, and after a long hesitation began to carve. For the next week he worked every day on his corner of the clock while Ula sculpted, in black walnut, the bird.

What Erich carved, not with the sure touch of years but with the eager hand of youth, was a little figure of Brangi. An old hound, lying asleep while the forest sprang and sang and quivered around him. A rough carving, a young carving, but even Erich could see that it was almost a good carving. His breath came fast as he realized that his hand had put the final touch to Old Ula's masterpiece.

Meanwhile Ula fashioned a slender bird with smoky gray feathers, barred on the breast with brown, tail tipped with white. He hinged the wings and the head. When he came to the feet, he did not, as other clockmakers were accustomed to do (as he himself had done in the past), stick the legs in the platform on which the bird was to stand, not troubling to carve feet. The platform was already in the house, behind double doors from which the bird would emerge to tell the hour. It was equipped with a perch for gripping. Carefully Ula gave his bird the long toes of the true cuckoo, two in front and two behind. So, when the last touch of paint had been applied to the feathers and he placed the bird carefully on the workbench, it stood upright, on its own feet.

"My dear Erich," said Ula. "We have finished. We

have made our clock. All that remains is for the paint to dry on the bird, and we have made a clock for ourselves like no other in the world."

He looked at the small figure of Brangi among the wild creatures and smiled. "What a good choice. You, I think, are going to be an artist."

"Like you, Ula."

The old man smiled. "I think of myself as a craftsman. But you—yes, one day you will carve things more important than cuckoo clocks."

"But Ula—"

Ula lifted a hand, smiled again, and sat back in his rocker. "I know what I say. Play something for me, Erich. Something soft, a lullaby. . . ."

The door stood open. Spring had come to the Black Forest, melting deep snows from woods and fields and village, gentling the winds, licking fringes of icicles from the eaves. They could feel the earth breathing softly after its long frozen sleep.

Erich took up the fiddle and played.

Kuckuk, Kuckuk, ruft's aus dem Wald. . . .

Dark gathered as Erich the Foundling played the fiddle and Old Ula listened with his eyes closed. They forgot that Erich was late, was long since due back at the Manor House to commence his chores.

Chores. The Manor House. What did those mean to these two on this day?

As Erich played, there came, from the shadowed corner where the workbench stood, a wavering, uncertain bird call.

Old Ula sat upright. Erich stood with the bow and fiddle dangling in his hands. Brangi got slowly to his feet and stared into the shadows.

They made no sound or sign, as the bird-song strengthened and became a series of every song known to the birds of the Black Forest.

"Are we awake, Ula?" asked Erich. "Are we in our dream somehow, or awake?"

"Awake, Erich. Awake! *We have dreamed our bird to life.* What a strange strange thing to have done!"

Ula got up and walked slowly toward the workbench, leaned over, and lit the lamp. He stood looking at the wooden cuckoo that sang like a mockingbird. Erich and Brangi followed and stood beside him.

"Let us see," said Old Ula softly, "if he will go into his house."

He picked the bird up in gentle hands, carried it to the clock that now hung on the wall, and pulled up the weights on their brass chains. Opening the little double doors, he held the bird up on his finger. "There," he said. "There is your home."

With a flick of its tail, the bird hopped inside, and the doors closed behind it.

Old Ula gripped Erich's hand. "Wait," he said. "It is almost six o'clock. Let us see what happens when the hour arrives."

They stood together in silence, and at six o'clock, with a whirring as the gong train was set in motion, the doors flew open, and the bird emerged on its platform and called, "Cuckoo . . . cuckoo . . . cuckoo . . . cuckoo . . . cuckoo . . . cuckoo." Then it disappeared behind the doors as they snapped shut.

"Just like any cuckoo clock," said Erich. "I think we had a dream, Ula. That was it. A dream."

"Listen, Erich!"

From inside the house they heard it again, that singing. Faint, then louder, lower, then higher.

"Ah," said Ula. "I believe he is going about his house, inspecting it, as any new householder would."

"Of course!" cried Erich. "Oh, he is going to love it, Ula. A bird never had such a home before as our bird has."

He pictured it going about the downstairs room, sitting in the rocker by the fireplace. Would the silk fires cast shadows on the wall as Old Ula's fire was casting them on the walls out here? He could almost see as the bird pecked

at his loaf of wooden bread, his wooden mug of chocolate. He would go upstairs, too, and find there his nice little bed with the white counterpane, his little lamp and tiny Bible on the table next to it.

"I wish we could be in there with him," said Erich, and the doors of the clock opened. Out flew the bird to land on Brangi's head. Brangi lifted heavy eyes, sighed, and settled again as the bird began its repertory of songs.

"It is a thank-you note, I believe," said Ula. "He is singing us his thanks."

"Yes," breathed Erich. "Yes, that must be it."

Being very old and very young, Ula and Erich had no difficulty in accepting a miracle when it was right there singing in the room with them. Only Brangi found it odd to have a bird on his head.

Erich said, when the bird had grown silent again, "He can come out of his house, but he will not be able to go back in unless the doors are opened for him."

"I shall open them, in the morning. Let him stay out here with Brangi and me for this night. It is late, Erich, and no doubt Frau Goddhart will have noticed your absence."

Erich said nothing. Frau Goddhart would most certainly have noticed his absence, and punishment was sure to follow. But no punishment could dim the marvel of this day with Ula and their clock and the wooden bird that sang.

"Still," Old Ula continued, "I would like you to do something for me. I would like you to bring Herr Goddhart here."

"Now? Tonight? *Herr* Goddhart?"

"Yes, Erich," Ula said firmly. "Herr Goddhart, as soon as you can bring him. And you are to come back with him. Tell him that I asked. He will understand."

Erich hung the fiddle and bow on the wall, looked at his old friend for a long time, then at the bird nestled on Brangi's head. Then he started for the Manor House.

He ran all the way.

"Ah, so there you are!" cried Frau Goddhart when he sped breathless into the great hall. "And what excuse do you have this time?"

As he had never been late before, and never had had an excuse before, Erich did not know how to answer. He turned to Herr Goddhart. "Papa," he said. "Herr Ula wishes you to come to him."

Erich was not only encouraged, he was required, to call the Goddharts Mama and Papa, showing the village that no difference was made between Frau Goddhart's own children and the waif of God she had taken under her protection. He was happy to call Herr Goddhart Papa, and usually managed not to call Frau Goddhart anything.

Now Frau Goddhart said, "Old Ula's dying at last, that must be it. And of course he wants me, not you," she told her husband.

Erich caught his breath. Somehow he was not surprised. Old Ula had waited to finish the clock, and now it was finished and he wanted to rest. Old Ula, he knew, was tired. Very tired. Still, the tears fell down his cheeks as he repeated, "Papa, he asked for *you* to come to him, and he wants me to go with you."

"Out of the question," Frau Goddhart said.

"My dear," said Herr Goddhart. "Erich says he asked for me—"

"A mistake. On Erich's part."

"Still, I will go to him. Erich will come with me," he added firmly.

A silence, and then Frau Goddhart said, "I shall accompany you. Old Ula would be much dismayed were I to fail him at this hour."

The carriage was brought around and, after a moment's indecision, Frau Goddhart gestured to Erich to climb in with them. He had never been in a carriage before, and as it jolted along at a great rate of speed he even forgot for a moment where he was going, and why.

It was a moonless, starless night. Shadows lunged before them, fell sideways, in the light of the carriage lamps. The horses' hooves on the cobbles struck sparks, and he had to clutch a handstrap as they swayed from side to side. It was exciting to be going through the dark in such a transport.

But at Ula's cottage, the fire and the lamp had burned low, and the spring evening coming through the open door was cold now. Erich, who had never been happy except in this room, found out about sorrow here.

While Herr Goddhart turned up the lamp and put a log on the fire and closed the door against the night, Erich sat silently on the rug beside Brangi, looking at his teacher and friend. He wanted to say something, but Frau Goddhart was talking so much, and she did not like to be interrupted.

Ula, however, from his rocking chair, held up a silencing hand. "I am weary, Frau Goddhart, and cannot listen. I wish to speak."

"Well, I never in my—"

Old Ula continued, looking at Herr Goddhart. "I asked you to come here because I wish to give something to Erich and feared there might be a—misunderstanding, unless I made clear that I am giving him this gift."

He thought Frau Goddhart would say I'd taken something, Erich said to himself. He did not know what Old Ula planned to give him. He did not care at all. What Ula was taking from him was everything he cared about. The times in this room, working together, eating and talking together, studying. Learning so much, not only from lessons.

This day, this day—when the carved bird flew and sang and they had found it not strange . . . only miraculous.

This day!

Ula was taking it all away, taking himself away, and Erich did not care what gift was left behind.

He looked around now for the bird, but there was no sign of it. Nine o'clock came, and the longcase made a deep statement, but no bird emerged from the fabulous cuckoo clock. Looking anxiously into Ula's face, he saw a faint twinkle and a nod of the bearded head toward Brangi. He leaned over, and sure enough, there between Brangi's paws, hidden by their size from the casual glance, nestled the wooden bird, as if under its mother's wing.

"Erich," said Old Ula in a hoarse soft voice, "go to the workbench and take up my leather case, the one with my best tools, and keep it with you, because you are going

---

47

to be an artist, and an artist must have the finest tools."

"Herr Ula!" Frau Goddhart cried out, "You cannot mean to give this boy a gift so valuable! He will not know how to take care of them. He will lose them, or misuse them. Surely it would be wiser if I were to—"

"Now take the fiddle and the bow from the wall," Ula continued, looking at Erich. "Good. Put them in their case. Keep that with you, too, because you love music, and you learned how to play on that fiddle. And now, come here."

Erich, holding the soft leather sack in one hand and the fiddle case in the other, approached the rocking chair. He leaned over, and without asking permission, put a kiss on his friend's wrinkled face.

"That's good, that's good," said Old Ula, patting his hand. "You have been my friend, Erich. Now, off you go."

Erich ran for the door.

"Erich!" Frau Goddhart called. "Remember, please, your manners! You have not thanked Herr Ula for—"

"He does not wish to thank me," said Ula. "He feels I am taking away so much more than I am giving. I am not really taking anything from him, but he will have to learn that for himself, in time. Goodbye, Erich."

"Goodbye," said Erich, walking out of the cottage without looking back.

He walked slowly across the village to the Manor House, climbed to his attic room, and sat holding the fiddle case and the soft leather case of fine tools.

He sat up all night, and in the morning heard the church bells begin to toll.

Except for Erich, all those whom Old Ula had loved and been loved by—his wife, the friends of his youth and age—were gone. But he was a man much respected in the village, and everyone came to his funeral.

Baron Balloon sent a wagon drawn by two black horses with plumes, and he himself arrived with the Baroness and Britt in his carriage with its span of gray horses, its imposing coat of arms. Other carriages drew up behind his, and those who did not have such equipage walked.

From Munich came Old Ula's great-nephew, who had inherited the little cottage and its contents. A rush of consolers greeted him. He nodded mournfully but was not inconsolable. He had scarcely known his great-uncle, yet here was this snug little cottage with its furnishings, all his. He would refer to it, back in Munich, as his "chalet in the Black Forest." That had a fine ring and even allayed his grievance at having to provide a buffet meal for a lot of people he did not know.

It was the custom to provide a feast, in this case modest, after the services in the churchyard were over. He had asked the Baron and Baroness, the Goddharts, the mayor, the priest, and some others of consequence to share it with him. They had all accepted gladly. A funeral made for an interesting gathering, especially after it was over.

Brangi, when he observed from his corner all these arrivals, lowered his head, opened his jaws, and gently took the bird into his large mouth. Then he lay quite still as people came and went, talked, sniffled a little, and reminisced, as is done on these occasions. Some even shed a few real tears.

Brangi lay quietly as Old Ula's coffin was carried out and placed on the wagon drawn by the black, plumed horses. He remained where he was as the procession started for the churchyard. Erich, who had not been invited to ride in the Goddharts' carriage—it being quite full of Goddharts—remained on the step of the cottage and watched the cortege as it moved away.

Then he glanced upward, and saw an amazing sight. It was Ula, ascending to heaven. A lot of birds were going with him, and it all looked very joyous.

Accustomed to remaining silent, except with Herr Goddhart or Old Ula himself, Erich did not cry out. But he looked eagerly into the faces of the villagers going past. He looked at the priest and the mayor, at the Baron and Baroness with beautiful Britt sitting between them. He looked at the Goddharts, at other important persons passing in their coaches. Then he scanned the faces of the

villagers walking by. The grown-up faces. The faces of children. But no one was looking up, and no one appeared to see this bright and glorious sight. For a long time Erich watched, until Old Ula and the birds were just specks against the sun. Then he dropped his gaze and sat on the steps, where he had so often sat with Ula, feeling, as he had so often felt with Ula, quite happy.

No one else had looked up, he guessed, because Old Ula had meant only for him, Erich the Foundling, to see the wonderful sight.

When all the people had gone, he wandered back into the cottage to look for the bird, but there was no sign of it. Perhaps Ula had somehow managed to get up and open the doors during the night and let the bird into its house? He went and stood beneath the clock, listening. There was no singing, however faint, to be heard. The half hour came, and then the hour, and the longcase clock took note, but no bird emerged from the cuckoo clock.

Erich could not understand it. Unless the bird had been one of those flying to heaven with Ula?

He looked at Brangi in the corner, and Brangi, though he thumped his tail briefly, gave no sign. He did not stir at all. Erich went and sat beside him, wondering about the bird and thinking about Ula, who by now must be in heaven itself.

When the nephew from Munich and the important people he had invited to the modest buffet meal returned, Frau Goddhart shot a glance at Erich. This was what came of befriending an unwanted infant. She found herself burdened with a bone-lazy, ungrateful, *sly* creature she could in no way get rid of. He had not even bothered to follow the procession to the churchyard. Wishing she could order Erich from the cottage, from the Manor House, from the village itself, she smiled at the great-nephew.

"There in the corner, beside the dog," she said, "is a waif I took into my home and my heart. I have thought of him as one of my own," she added, almost choking. "He was greatly attached to your uncle."

"Great-uncle."

"Of course."

She did not add that the great-uncle had been attached to Erich. Not necessary to bother a man from Munich with trifles. And perhaps it was not entirely true? Old Ula had found the boy useful these past years. In his disordered condition, he had overpaid with that case of fine tools and the fiddle. She did not see why her own children should not have these things, since save for her indulgence in allowing the boy to come here each day, Old Ula would not have benefited from so much free help. The more she thought, the surer she was that Old Ula had not been in his proper senses to give such valuable things to Erich the Foundling. She would have to see about this, as soon as they were home.

Meanwhile, the great-nephew was being gracious to his guests while taking note of what the cottage contained. He had already been upstairs and had seen the fine four-post bed. Excellent, excellent. The longcase clock, not made by his uncle, was one of the finest he had ever seen. He would take it to Munich with him. But, most of all, his attention was on that extraordinary cuckoo clock. He had never seen anything to match it. He looked at it with such happy greed that at once all eyes were on it. Exclamations of wonder crowded the air.

Such a clock! Such a thing of intricately, delicately, exquisitely carved beauty not one in the room had ever seen before.

Baron Balloon swelled with covetousness. He swept the room with his gaze, seeking a likely collaborator. His glance hesitated on Frau Goddhart, who would say anything he wanted her to, then alighted on Erich, huddled in the corner.

"Come here, boy," he said gruffly. "Come and stand beside me. Now, you were Old Ula's assistant, were you not?" He fixed Erich with his hard eyes. "Answer me!"

"I came here. I helped him."

"Speak up! Speak up! You were here, right in this room, when I came to order the finest cuckoo clock in the world—which this clearly is—for my daughter's birthday, were you not?"

Erich looked at the Baron, at the great-nephew, at Frau Goddhart. "Yes," he said. "I was here." The Baron Balloon, he realized, was telling the truth. He *had* ordered such a clock, and Erich had been here when he did so.

"He's a child," the great-nephew said angrily. "I will not take the word of a child."

Frau Goddhart spoke up. "Ah . . . but he told *me*," she said, with a satisfied glance at the Baron. "I distinctly recall that Erich came to me and said, 'Mama, the Baron has ordered the finest clock in the world to be made for his daughter's birthday.' Yes, yes. I recall it clearly."

Erich stared at her, dumbstruck.

"Did no one else hear of this?" said the great-nephew,

faltering. He might not believe the boy, but did not see how he dared doubt the imposing Frau Goddhart.

"That is my clock!" said the Baron.

"But surely, Herr Baron," said the great-nephew, "it was my great-uncle's clock, since there it is, on his wall. Therefore, you understand, it now belongs to me."

"I ordered it," said the Baron firmly, "for my daughter's birthday, which is to be in a few days. It is mine."

The great-nephew was beginning to get red in the face. He had no intention of parting with the clock, even to a Baron. "Can you provide me with anything to prove what you say? A note, a bit of writing, something to show that you did, indeed, order this particular clock?"

"Are you questioning my word?" the Baron bellowed.

After a moment's reflection, the great-nephew nodded. "I believe I am. Yes, I am."

All assembled listened with interest. Certainly no one around here had ever questioned the Baron Balloon's word. It showed how grand people from Munich considered themselves to be. A great-nephew of a poor clockmaker standing up to a Baron! On the whole, everyone except the Baron and Frau Goddhart was gratified. As for her, she was furious. An insult to the Baron, in her view, was as good as an insult to the Goddharts. It was not to be tolerated.

"I have said nothing about this before," she told the company, "because Erich told me it was a secret. He always comes to me with his little secrets. This, of course, was a *big* secret, but he comes to me with his big secrets, too." She smiled severely at Erich, who was staring at her, his mouth open. "You do recall telling me about the clock, do you not, my boy?"

Erich was now ten years old. With Old Ula gone, he was without a friend, save Herr Goddhart. But just as Frau Goddhart said what the Baron wished her to, so Herr Goddhart always said what Frau Goddhart wished him to. Besides, there had been no one here except Erich when Old Ula refused to make a clock for the Baron. Who would take the word of a waif for that?

He nodded.

"Speak up!" said Baron Balloon and Frau Goddhart at once.

"Yes," said Erich.

"Yes, *what?*" said the Baron. "Speak louder, so we can all hear you!"

"I told Frau—I mean, Mama—I told her about the clock." He went back to sit beside Brangi, trembling from the effort of telling a lie. How often had Old Ula talked about the beauty of truth. He had never said how ugly a lie felt on the tongue. Erich supposed that was because Old Ula had not told lies.

The great-nephew from Munich was giving in. "Very well, Herr Baron. How much was my uncle to be paid for this clock?"

Baron Balloon looked at the ceiling and named a sum at which everyone, even Frau Goddhart, looked astonished. The meanest intelligence could see that the clock was worth much much more than the figure the Baron offered. "That was only a down payment, of course," he added hastily.

"But you have not paid even that," said the great-nephew. "There is no money in the house at all. I have looked."

"No, no," said the Baron, ruddy with rage. "I was to pay when it was completed."

"Then you can pay me," said the great-nephew. "The down payment which you did not pay down, and—" He named a huge additional sum, at which the Baron's eyes popped.

Just then Britt, who had been out in the garden playing, entered the cottage. Her eye fell immediately on the clock. "Papa! Mama!" she cried. "Oh, look at the beautiful, beautiful clock! That is the most lovely thing I ever did see in my life!"

The clock that Fritz had carved with many guns and dead creatures was hanging in a passageway in the castle because Britt refused to have it in her room. But this clock! It sang! It sang with beauty! "How lovely it is," she said again.

"It is yours, my darling. I had it made especially for you," said her father.

Now Erich did not feel quite so bad about having told a lie. Britt was happy. It seemed to Erich that it was good for Britt to feel happy.

"Be quiet, everyone!" the Baron ordered. "It approaches noon. Now we shall see what fine bird old Ula made for my —that is, for *his* masterpiece."

Twelve o'clock. The longcase clock chimed, boomed twelve times, fell silent. The company waited a minute, another minute, and yet one more, before the Baron strode over to the cuckoo clock, pried open the doors, and peered inside.

"There is no bird!" he cried out.

"No bird!" the mayor and the priest and the Goddharts

and the rest of the assorted important persons repeated in chorus.

"No bird?" sighed Britt.

Erich looked at Brangi in a puzzled way. The bird, the wooden bird that sang all the songs of the Black Forest, had been here with the three of them, Old Ula, Brangi, and himself. They had seen it. They had heard it. Where was it now? He had looked everywhere, while the people were making their way to the churchyard, and it was not in the house. It must, he thought, have gone to heaven with Ula. And yet that seemed to him strange, not right. Old Ula would not want a clock of his to be here on earth un-completed. He especially would not want to take the bird away from the house he had so lovingly built for it.

"Brangi," he whispered. "Do you know where the bird is?"

Brangi thumped his tail.

So the Baron told the great-nephew that he could take the clock to Munich with him after all. What good was a cuckoo clock without a cuckoo? The great-nephew, quite put out at the loss of the large sum he'd demanded of the Baron, said that after all the house was more important than the bird, why didn't the Baron just have someone else make a cuckoo bird to go in it? Erich was thinking that no one would ever be able to make another bird for this house, since it had been made for one bird only, and Britt tugged at her father's sleeve and said that no matter what, she wanted that clock because it was the most beautiful thing she had ever seen.

The Baron and the great-nephew came to an agreement that satisfied neither, and then everyone began to eat and drink.

Erich, his hand on Brangi's head, looked thoughtfully at Frau Goddhart. Drawing a deep breath, he said in a clear and carrying voice, "Mama—Mama, may Brangi come to the Manor House—I mean, come home—with us? He is all alone now and will have no one to look after him."

Frau Goddhart licked a whipped-cream mustache from her upper lip, caught back a scowl, reminded herself that she was in the presence of all the people in the village who mattered. She looked at Brangi and said to herself that he was not long for this world anyway. Making one attempt to avoid taking the old dog, she said, "That is a kind thought, Erich, and does you credit. But Old Ula's great-nephew will surely want to have his great-uncle's dog, for sentiment's sake."

"No, no, my dear lady. The dog should stay with Erich and his loving guardians. I doubt if he could adjust to city life at his age. No, no. I should not dream of taking him."

"Very well," said Frau Goddhart. "Let him come. Not into the house, mind you," she warned Erich. Even the necessity of being publicly warm-hearted could not prevent her from adding that. The little wretch had timed his request to offer her no way of refusal, but he would learn not to take advantage of her again in this fashion.

Sly, sly. She would teach him.

The occasion was over. The great-nephew arranged for the longcase clock to be shipped to Munich. The guests departed as he prepared to put a bolt on the cottage that had never been locked before. Baron Balloon and the Baroness and Britt and the birdless cuckoo clock set off in the Baron's carriage, up the winding road to the castle at the top of the mountain. The mayor and the priest and the other persons of consequence went to their homes. The Goddhart's carriage departed, full of Goddharts, and Erich and Brangi walked slowly through the village to the Manor House.

Erich took Brangi around to the kitchen yard, upended a wooden bucket, and sat on it to explain to the dog that he would have to remain outside all night.

"There is not any way," he pointed out, "that I could sneak you up to the attic, not even by the back stairs. You do understand?"

Brangi didn't nod, but it was clear that he comprehended the situation.

The back stairs, of course, were the only ones Erich used, but there was always someone else using them, too. One of the maids, the grooms, the cooks. While Erich did not think any of them would tell on him, he could not be absolutely sure. Especially he wasn't sure about Cook, who ruled the under-cooks in a manner both jolly and severe; no one ever knew which side of her nature would be uppermost.

("It depends on the sauce," one of the under-cooks had told Erich.

"The sauce?"

"If the sauce is perfection, there is no discord in our kitchens, *but*! Let anything go wrong with it, and Cook's disposition curdles and sours worse than the worst sauce you ever tasted.")

Now Erich looked down at the old dog and said, "I guess we'll have to pray for a successful sauce, since you must be very hungry. I am going to go in the kitchen and ask Cook if you can have a bone. With meat on it."

He got up, then stopped as Brangi leaned over and put his chin to the ground. The lamplight from the kitchen, streaming out of the window and onto the earthen yard, fell upon the bird as Brangi carefully released it from his mouth.

"Brangi!" Erich gasped. "You've been hiding him all this time!" He stooped down to see if any damage had come to the cuckoo from its sojourn in the dog's mouth. No. It was neat and trim as if fresh from the nest, and it stood motionless between Brangi's paws.

Carefully, Erich picked it up, expecting—hoping—that it would stir and flutter in his hand. Again, no. It lay on his palm, beautiful and unmoving. Quite wooden.

Erich sighed. He supposed that the magic had gone with Old Ula. Not for a moment did he think that he and Ula and Brangi had imagined the magic. The bird had flown. It had sung. They three had seen its flight and heard its songs. Old Ula had counted thirty-six different calls. And all this had happened in the cottage only a few nights before.

Standing, he put the bird in one of the pockets of his

smock. Then, with another pat for Brangi, he went into the huge kitchen to ask Cook for a bone.

"A big one, with meat on it," he said, when he'd got the cook's attention.

"Oh, my. What an order! A big bone with meat on it. And do you expect me just to hand it to you, Erich? The mistress knows every scrap in her kitchen, down to a mustard seed. How should I explain the absence of a big bone with meat on it?"

"But she said I could bring Brangi home with me. And he is hungry."

"Well then, you go and ask the mistress yourself if you may have a bone for your dog, since I will not take it upon myself to release even a little bone with no meat on it."

Erich nodded glumly, and went in search of Frau Goddhart. He wandered down the long passageway that led from the kitchens to the great hall, where he found Herr Goddhart and Frau Goddhart sitting in silence in high carved chairs. Occasional small noises, quickly muffled, could be heard from the six Goddhart children upstairs, but here in the hall there was no sound except for Frau Goddhart's breathing as she worked on her tapestry. Herr Goddhart was turning his pipe around in his hands. This was not the hour at which he stepped outside to smoke it. Erich thought of Old Ula, lighting up whenever he wished to, outdoors or indoors, as he pleased.

Now, not observing Erich in the shadows, Frau Goddhart said to her husband, "He must be paid out for thrusting that dog upon me. He's sly, that one. Oh, sly . . ."

"But, my dear, you agreed—"

"He asked at such a time and in such a manner as to allow me no choice." Frau Goddhart waited for comment, got none, and continued. "I will not be taken advantage of in this fashion. Sly, sly. I cannot abide slyness. Honesty, openness, these are the qualities of *our* children. But from the beginning that urchin has taken advantage of my kindness. Why do you not reply?" she said loudly.

Herr Goddhart turned his pipe about, consulting it.

"Do you not agree with me?" his wife demanded.

"Well . . . not entirely," said the small man, his jaw set.

"Oh, you are a fool, a ninny. You have been taken in by him all these years. . . . Well, not I. When he comes back—where is he, by the by?"

"I do not know, my dear."

"Dawdling. Wasting my time. There are twelve pair of boots to be blacked by morning. The simple little tasks I give him, in exchange for a place in our home and our hearts, and he forgets even those!"

"Perhaps he has gone right to his attic. Perhaps he is grieving for Old Ula."

"Grieving! He did not even go to the churchyard!"

"But those who did go to the churchyard were not grieving. Perhaps the boy and the dog who remained in the cottage were Old Ula's only real mourners."

"Twaddle!" Frau Goddhart put her needle aside. "If he is up in his attic, you must go and tell him to give you the fiddle and the sack of tools."

"But no!" Herr Goddhart protested. "Those were given to him by Old Ula. In our presence!"

"An old man, wandering in his wits. He did not know what he was saying. Those things, the fine tools, the fiddle, are far too good for a foundling, and I will not allow him to have them. Just think what such things will mean to *our* children!"

"But none of them is interested in carving, and none of them is musical. Besides," Herr Goddhart said stubbornly, "they were given to Erich."

"No more!" said Frau Goddhart. "I will have those tools and that fiddle! Small enough repayment for all the years of shelter and food and kindness the foundling has received at our hands. Go and tell him! And if he is not there, take them!"

Erich turned and raced down the hall, up the back stairs to the room in the attic that had been his only home. He took the soft leather case of tools, thrust it into the second pocket of his smock, took the fiddle in its case, and started from the room. But then he turned and looked sadly at the books Herr Goddhart had given him. He wished he could stay to say goodbye to Herr Goddhart. Well, maybe one day, when he was safely away, he could write a letter, thanking him for being gentle.

He sped down the back stairs again before Herr Goddhart, going slowly up the front staircase, could arrive at the attic floor.

In the kitchen, Cook was not to be seen. Erich supposed she had gone to the pantry for something. But lying on the huge wooden table was a fine great bone with meat on it, and a little bone with almost no meat on it. He supposed that Cook had got them out and was waiting to see which was to be given to Brangi. He also supposed that the sauce tonight had turned out wonderfully well, or she'd not have got out any bones at all.

Snatching up the big one, he was out in the kitchen yard in a moment, whispering in Brangi's ear. "Come along," he said urgently. "Come with me, Brangi. We are off to seek our fortune!"

In those days it was not unusual for a boy Erich's age to run off to seek his fortune. Younger sons, neglected for older ones. Stepsons flying from ill-treatment. Orphans and foundlings. Boys even younger would leave unhappy homes and go into the wide world seeking their fortunes, which, according to the stories, they always found.

So Erich and Brangi walked away from the Manor House, the one carrying his fiddle, the other his bone.

They came to the foot of the mountain at the top of which was the castle of the Baron Balloon. Erich stood a long time looking at the road winding upwards. Then he turned to Brangi and said, "Come into this thicket here, and lie down with your bone. I am going up to the castle to try to find Britt and return the bird to its home. I know it will sing again if only it can be in its own house."

Brangi would have followed Erich up the mountain, but it was a long way up and a long way down and he was tired and hungry. He lay down gratefully.

Erich put the fiddle beside him. "Guard it, Brangi, and wait for me." He looked up at the mountain again. "I shall probably be a long time going up and a long time coming down, so be patient, and do not make a sound."

He moved the branches so that Brangi was quite concealed, and started up to the castle.

It was near daybreak when Erich arrived at the castle and wandered around it wondering how to find Britt. He had not realized how vast a construction a castle was. The Manor House seemed small in comparison, and Ula's cottage a toy little larger than one of his own cuckoo clocks.

He was starting around for the second time when Britt herself leaned out of a window and called, "Erich! *Psst!* Up here!"

Erich looked about, looked up, scanned the walls, and finally located Britt leaning way out of a little window in a tower. He stood smiling at her. It seemed quite right to him that Britt should live in a tower.

"What are you doing here?" she called down in a clear, soft voice.

"Looking for you!" he yelled.

"Oh, do hush. Not so loud. Wait there. I'll be down."

She vanished from the window, and Erich sat on the grass and watched the sun lift clear of the distant mountains. Even now in spring the tops of the peaks were covered with snow. Their satiny slopes were drizzled gold by the morning sun. Erich was thinking how beautiful it was and how hungry he was when Britt ran across the lawn, light as a blown veil. She beckoned to him.

"Quickly, quickly!" she said. "Come around to the side."

Erich followed her as she pushed through a stand of yew bushes to a small door concealed from view. Opening it, she turned and beckoned again and they started climbing a winding stone staircase.

"It's a secret passage," she told him. "The castle is full of secret passages. This one is mine, and I think it really is a secret. I found it by accident when I was hiding behind the big tapestry in my room one day."

"Why were you hiding?"

"I have tantrums."

"Oh."

Erich had never personally had a tantrum, but knew what they were from watching the Goddhart children. "Why?" he asked.

"Because they won't let me go out and play with other children. And they won't let me out of the castle at all when the gypsies are camping in the fields. So I was hiding. To scare them, you know. And I leaned against the wall and a panel opened right into this stone stairway. Isn't it wonderful?"

Erich thought it awfully damp and dark and cold, but agreed it would be wonderful if you wanted to get out when people said you had to stay in.

They were through the panel at the back of the tapestry and then into Britt's room. Oh, what a beautiful apartment it was, with the morning sun shining on furniture all painted and carved, on bright cushions and soft carpets and bowls of flowers. Erich looked about him in a daze. He had never seen the rooms of the Goddhart children, but was sure they could be nothing like this.

And there, by itself on one wall, hung Old Ula's clock. It looked more wonderful up here on the mountaintop even than it had on the cottage wall down in the valley. Erich supposed that was because it was dark down there. Up here, it seemed to him, it would be like living east of the sun.

"Now," said Britt, sitting on a big cushion, "tell me why you came up here. Sit, sit," she said, pointing to a cushion close by.

Erich slapped at his clothes uncertainly. "I have been walking for a long time. I think I am dusty."

"Oh, what does that matter? Sit *down*, Erich, and tell me why you walked all the way up the mountain. To see me?" she said with a quick smile.

"To give you something."

Britt looked surprised. How could Erich the Foundling have anything to give to her, the Baron's daughter? She already had everything. Then, seeing him look at the clock, she cried, "Erich! You have made a bird for my clock! I know it! Oh, how clever you are!"

"No, no, no," said Erich, frowning. "*I* did not make it. Ula made it, before he went to heaven—" He hesitated, wondering whether to tell Britt how he had seen Old Ula and the birds ascending through the sky and had watched until they were just specks against the sun. He decided not to. He felt sure that Ula had meant only for him to see the miracle.

"Ula made the cuckoo," he said, "but then he did not have a chance to put it back in the clock—"

"Back in?" said Britt. "He put it in and then took it out again?"

"It flew out."

Britt burst into laughter. "You are *funny*, Erich. You always look so thin and solemn. I *never* would have dreamed you were funny."

Erich took the bird from the pocket of his smock and held it out to her.

She took the wooden bird and turned it about, carefully examining each carved feather, marveling at the perfect feet, at the lift of the head and the long eyes. "It is a lovely, beautiful bird," she said. "And I know it belongs in my clock. But I do not think," she added, her eyes sparkling, "that it will fly there."

She seemed to be right. The bird lay cupped in her hands, unmoving.

"Well," said Erich at length. "I guess we will have to put it in."

He walked to the clock, opened the double doors, and put the carved cuckoo on its perch. The doors closed. Erich, pulling on the chains that would set the two trains in motion—one for the works, the other for the gong and bellows—wondered if the bird would even emerge to tell the time.

They would find out, presently.

———

Meanwhile, dizzy with hunger, he sank down on a yellow cushion and closed his eyes.

"Are you tired?" Britt asked.

He nodded.

"Are you hungry?"

"Oh, yes. Very."

"I have a chunk of chocolate and some biscuits here. Would you like those?"

Erich's eyes flew open and he sat up. "Yes," he said. "I would like those."

After he had eaten and had a drink of cool water, he began to feel himself again. All the way up the mountain he had been, it seemed to him, wandering in a mist. He was lonely for Ula, alarmed at running away to seek his fortune, tired and very hungry, and he had not really been paying heed to what he was doing.

Now, sustained by food, he concluded that he was actually talking to the daughter of the Baron and Baroness Balloon, in her room. He did not think they would be pleased, nor would Frau Goddhart, if they knew.

"I think I had better leave," he said, jumping up.

"Oh, but you cannot! Not until the hour, so that we can see whether the bird you made is going to tell time for me."

"I did not make it!" Erich cried out. "It was Ula that made it! I could not make anything so fine, so wonderful."

"Well, maybe not," Britt conceded. "Not yet. Give me your hand, Erich."

"My hand?"

"I am going to tell your fortune from your palm. I learned from the gypsies."

"I thought you were not allowed out when the gypsies are about."

"I said they would not let me out. I didn't say I did not *get* out. I have been going to see the gypsies for years. I love them. Your hand, Erich."

She had a commanding way that Erich guessed came of being a Baron's daughter. He put out his hand, ashamed at how dirty it was.

Britt did not seem to notice. She bent over his palm, tracing lines here and there, nodding to herself and muttering. Finally she looked up. "Just as I thought."

"What?" Erich asked uneasily.

"You are going to be famous."

"I am?"

"You are going to be a great artist. And you will not only make marvelous clocks, but splendid carvings—reredos for cathedrals, and screens for queens and empresses, and statues for kings and emperors. . . ."

Erich looked at his grimy hand. "How can you see all that in there?"

"I can. The gypsies say I have the touch."

"Ula said I was going to be an artist," Erich said softly.

"There, you see! But tell me, where are you going when you leave here?"

"Through the Black Forest. I think Frau Goddhart will send riders looking for me, but she will send them along the highway. I do not think they will go through the woods."

"Why would she send anyone after you, Erich? I do not think Frau Goddhart is at all so kind as she tries to

make us believe. Do you think she *cares* for you and will want you back?"

"I took the tools and the fiddle that Ula gave me. She cares for those and will want them back."

"But if Ula gave them to you—"

"She said his wits were scattered and that he did not really mean me to have them."

"Well, he really did," Britt said firmly. "I know."

Erich wondered if the gypsies had given her the second sight, as well as teaching her to read the future in a person's hand. Still, he was quite sure, within himself, that Ula had meant for him to have the tools and the fiddle. And Ula would be glad, too, that he and Brangi were together now.

He looked at the clock. Five minutes until the hour. "As soon as it strikes, I must get back to Brangi, who is waiting for me at the foot of the mountain."

Would it strike? They'd know soon now.

"Brangi is going with you?" Britt asked.

"Yes."

"But he is so old. Surely he will not be able to go far?"

"He wants to be with me. We will go as far as we can together, and then when he can go no further, I will wait with him while he goes to sleep."

"I see." Britt sighed. "Well, you must stay a little longer, after the clock strikes"—Britt now seemed confident that the bird would come out of its house on time and announce the hour—"after it has proved itself, I will go down to the kitchens and get some food for you and Brangi, for the start of your journey."

Erich could not say no to that.

They waited in silence the last two minutes.

Erich could feel the movement of his heart. It thumped against his ribs as if asking to be let out. And then he felt a rush of joy, as the whirring commenced that signified the appearance of the bird.

Six o'clock.

The double doors flew open, the bird on his perch slid into view, and six times he called, "Cuckoo . . . cuckoo . . . cuckoo . . . cuckoo . . . cuckoo . . . cuckoo. . . ."

The bird slid backward, the doors closed.

Britt clasped her hands. "Oh, Erich, it is wonderful, your bird! I love it!"

"But, *please*—"

"Very well, then. Old Ula's bird. But to me it feels like your bird, Erich." She began to hum. *"Kuckuk, Kuckuk, ruft's aus dem Wald . . ."*

Erich, standing beneath the clock, heard another song. "Fraulein Britt," he said softly. "Come here and listen."

"Listen?" she said, skipping to his side. "Listen to what?"

From within the house, Erich could hear the songs of the wooden bird, all his thirty-six Black Forest variations. *That is because he is happy to be home*, Erich thought. He imagined the bird going from place to place in his little house, singing with joy.

"Listen to what?" Britt asked again. "What am I supposed to hear? I don't hear anything."

"Nothing?"

Britt tipped her head. Outside, the birds were singing aubades—morning songs—in the trees.

"The bird-songs?" she said.

"Yes! Is it not strange and marvelous?"

"Well, I always like to hear the birds singing, but it is not so very strange, Erich. They always sing in the morning in the spring."

Erich nodded. "Yes, of course," he said. It was true. . . . Only for Ula and Brangi and himself had the carved bird sung his songs. Now it would never fly out of its house again, and though it sang, no one would hear it. It would stay home and tell the hours and be, for all the world knew, just a bird in a cuckoo clock. A beautiful bird in a beautiful clock, but nothing more.

Britt went behind the tapestry and down the winding stairway to the kitchen, where she made up a basket of food for Erich to take on the first stage of his journey. Bread and cheese and knockwurst and apples and nuts and chocolate and ginger cookies. She put in something of everything she could find, covered the basket with a linen napkin, and then, before the cooks arrived, sped back up the secret stairway.

"There," she said. "That should keep you and Brangi for days. And then what will you do?" she asked anxiously.

"I can always offer to chop wood or black boots or scrub pots in houses that we pass, enough for us to get supper."

"But you will keep going?"

"Yes. We will keep going."

"Until when?"

"Until I find my fortune. I expect something will happen that will tell me where to stop."

"Will you come back?"

"I do not think so," he said hesitantly.

"But I would like you to come back, Erich. Someday, a long time from now, when you are a great artist."

"Why do you want me to come back?" he asked.

"Because I like you."

Erich smiled. "Then I shall come back."

"But now . . . now you must go. It is a long way down the mountain, and Brangi will be waiting for you."

When Britt showed the Baron and Baroness Balloon the bird in the clock, she was careful to say that Erich the Foundling had only brought it up the mountain to her, and that Old Ula had actually made it.

Erich, she knew, would want her to make this clear.

Still, somehow word got around the village that Erich himself had carved the bird and caused it to call the hours and that was why the clock was whole again.

"Fancy that," people said. "A foundling. And so young. To finish his master's work so masterfully. It is indeed a wonder."

Of course, the entire village was aware that Erich was gone from the Manor House. There was much talk. Some said Frau Goddhart's kindness had been sadly repaid, and some said it was her kindness that had finally driven him away. All were agreed that he was ungrateful and bound to become a fine artist.

Many people came to see the marvel of the clock, including, of course, Frau Goddhart. The sight of it filled her with rage, though she managed to smile sadly and even touched a tear with her lace-bordered handkerchief.

"How I miss the lad," she said to the Baroness, who was serving tea.

"Surely his departure was sudden?" said the Baroness.

Frau Goddhart looked even sadder. "Without a word to us, who have been mother and father to him. Oh, the ingratitude of it makes my heart ache. He is also a thief," she went on in a voice all at once flinty. "He took some valuable tools and a violin that Old Ula intended for my children—"

"What a wicked boy he must be. Although Britt says—"

"And what does your beautiful daughter say? Anything he said about me was a lie."

"Dear lady, he did not mention you." Or, if he had, Britt had not mentioned that. "It was what she said about him I had reference to."

"And what was that?"

"Why, Britt says she had a vision that Erich the Foundling is going to be a famous and great artist. She says he is going to make clocks for queens and screens for empresses. She says that kings and emperors will come to him, begging to have their busts styled. She says he is destined to make the reredos for the greatest cathedral in Europe."

"She said all that?"

"Yes. And she did sound as if she knew. I sometimes think Britt has the second sight, though where she gets it from I cannot think. The Baron and I," she said proudly, "have no powers of discernment."

Frau Goddhart could scarcely contain herself. Erich, that nameless waif whom she had taken in from the storm, was to be a great artist! And famous! And, no doubt, rich! Small chance he would think to give credit to the woman whose kind heart had made it all possible for him.

When she got back to the Manor House she tried to think of some way to blame everything on Herr Goddhart, but since she could not, she went to her room and had a tantrum.

Herr Goddhart stepped outside to smoke his pipe. He sat on a bench and watched the smoke drift away from him.

From the Black Forest came the call of the cuckoo, and on the chimneytops tall white storks came and went, clacking their long beaks together, making repairs to last year's nests.

Herr Goddhart looked and listened, but his thoughts were with Erich, wandering on his own in the wide world. He sighed deeply, and wondered if he and Erich would ever meet again.

These events took place many years in the past, and all the people in this story have gone to a world beyond the wide world where Erich sought, and found, his fortune long ago. The castle has crumbled, though a few walls still stand and the winding stone stairway is open to the sky, secret no longer. The village has become a city. It gulped up Old Ula's cottage, and the Manor House, and many houses besides. Much has changed. But still the storks come back from Africa in the springtime and build their nests atop chimneys. Still the cuckoo calls from the woods in springtime and snow lies on the mountaintops all year round.

There is, on a fine linden-lined street, an elegant apartment building, and on the wall of one of these apartments hangs Old Ula's clock. The people who found it, in an old shop on a side street, are very proud of it and show it off to visitors.

"A work of art, as you see," the man will say.

"All hand-carved," the wife points out.

"See," the man says, "see this little dog, down here in the corner? Carved by another hand, one can tell. Not so expert a hand."

"But it shows great promise, does it not?" his wife adds, "this little carving of the dog?"

Sometimes, even when visitors are not there, the man and his wife will sit down just before the hour arrives, to see their marvelous wooden cuckoo bird emerge from the double doors and flute his woodsy call.

The clock keeps perfect time.

In between the hours, the bird goes about his little house, sits in front of his hearth, where a silken fire casts shadows on the ceiling, pecks at his wooden loaf and his wooden mug of chocolate and his wooden ginger cookie. He goes upstairs to lie on his four-post bed

and look at his tiny Bible by the light of his little lamp.

And he sings! Oh, he sings all day, as he goes about his house, the thirty-six songs of the birds of the Black Forest, though no one ever hears a note except cuckoo . . . cuckoo . . . cuckoo. . . .

THE CUCKOO CLOCK

has been set on the Linotype by Maryland Linotype Composition Company, Baltimore, Maryland, in Primer, a typeface designed by the distinguished American artist Rudolph Ruzicka (1883–1978). Designed as a more elegant version of the American face Century Schoolbook, Primer is a transitional face between the classic sixteenth century faces and the more heavily contrasted faces of the late eighteenth century. Born in Bohemia, Ruzicka came to America in 1894 and worked for many years as a commercial wood engraver. He designed and illustrated many books, was proficient in a wide variety of graphic techniques, and was the creator of many typefaces still in everyday use.

The book has been printed and bound by Halliday Lithograph, West Hanover, Massachusetts. The paper is Glatfelter Offset, an entirely acid-free paper.

Designed by Barbara Dupree Knowles